A Second Mysterious Murder at West Egg!

Summer, 1926

All rights, including adaption for Film, TV, Stage or any form of internet screening, strictly reserved. No part of this publication may be reproduced (EXCEPT for the use of guests), stored in a retrieval system, or transmitted at any times by any means electronic, mechanical, photocopying, recording or otherwise without the prior permission of the copyright holder.

©Gareth Jones 2021

Please be nice.

Contents

Introduction	1
Instructions (not in role)	5
Invitations	12
Character Backstories	
John J Pilaster 111	14
Dolores Everhartt	15
Tony Biblioni (played by the host)	17
Carlotta Borlotti	18
Rafe Hardy	20
Julia Detvarmeg	21
Hamish McHammer	23
Irena Yaetosdelel	24
Hint cards	27 to 42
Menu	43
Other works by the author	45

Introduction

I've always been fascinated by Gatsby and the mid 1920's, so writing a murder mystery based in his sumptuous mansion seemed like a natural thing to do.

When I realised that friends of ours who lived on Long Island were minutes away from the supposed setting, the second part of the plan fell into place.

A photo of the view across the bay complete with a jetty and a white mansion, was achievable and could be printed on thin window-sized canvas to provide an authentic "view". This worked better than we could have possibly hoped because, as the sun set in our real street, it seemed to set in the picture.

Add to the mix a group of food and wine loving friends who would commit to dressing up and acting the part and we were ready to go... All I had to do was write it.

Covid 19 put us back a year but we got there in the end and had a fabulous time.

This book contains all that you need to stage your own evening, including a realistic menu of the time.

Photocopy anything that you need but please, only for your own use. Or, contact me at ghjmep@icloud.com and I'll send you the interior as a word file so that you can just print it (assuming that there aren't too many and I'm still able to).

I very much hope that you enjoy it!

Gareth

An Evening at West Egg

Jay Gatsby has "departed". His lavish mansion on Long Island, where you will be having dinner, is now owned by the Industrial Giant John J Pilaster 11. The slightly lesser Industrial Giant John J Pilaster 111, a Pillar of Long Island Society, and his glamorous second wife, the film star, Dolores Everhartt, will be there, but as guests since JJP 111 fell out with Daddy.

Daddy will be upstairs getting ready.

All of you will have been in the house and grounds all afternoon; swimming, playing tennis, boating on the lake, walking in the woods... JJP has not been seen since mid-afternoon... You will gather on the terrace at 6pm for drinks before dinner.

Standard 1920's type evening wear is fine for all characters, but you may choose to add little touches. The first part of the "evening" will be mingling and chatting to get to know each other a little better.

You all know of each other, but not how you know JJP11 (except the obvious, i.e., your partners and his family), except for Hamish McHammer. Hamish has won an enormous lottery win and is therefore both intriguing and mysterious.

Please arrive in character prepared to chat. You can ask questions about what people have been up to, the weather, issues they might be interested in etc. Your personal cards will give you ideas bit do feel free to improvise based on the information below.

NB: Staying in character all evening will, I think, be a strain, so the basic rule will be that when we are given the signal, we can be ourselves and not discuss the developing scenario.

The signal to show when we need to be in role will be Tony Biblioni putting on his dark glasses, which will be mainly between courses. Tony Biblioni will excuse himself after the oysters and return with the bad news...

Tony will be in charge of finding the killer, or killers, and therefore lead the evening (for this reason he should be played by the host).

He did considerable business with his "friend", who is now the victim. Everyone knows that the responsible person is in the room and nobody wants the Police involved. Tony will deal with all of that, once the "case" has been solved.

Here are some very brief notes so that you know something about each of the characters.

Irena
She was the mistress of the "about to be" deceased; cast off when he realised that her collection of Faberge Eggs, which he wanted for his West Egg Mansion, had been lost on the Titanic! This is a well-known scandal. Garbo based her acting persona on Irina... She is strangely fascinated with Hamish, who she has invited since JJP 11 generally ignores her anyway.

Hamish
Is a lottery winner and is now fabulously rich. He is the one that nobody really knows much about.

Carlotta
Carlotta Borlotti is also an actress, and full of beans. Although not quite so famous as Dolores, she does get "better" parts, often in gangster movies. She is there with Tony Biblioni.

Rafe
An English Actor type. Learnt Russian so that he could be authentic in his role as "Ivan the Terrible" and Norwegian so that he could play, "Thor", a part he never got. He is an author of best-selling, but not very good books. He has invited Julia because she asked him to. He sniffs a story.

Tony Biblioni
Is a book loving Mafiosi who enjoyed a brief period of fame when he appeared in "Get Santa" ... He has been "helping out" JJP Senior with some issues in the Labour unions who deliver concrete to build his vast SkyScrapers. No-one **directly** mentions his gangland role. He is interested in buying up the rights to Rafe's books, but no one is quite sure why.

JJP 111
Is a spoilt rich kid who doesn't really understand. Daddy

made all the money, all he has done is lose it. Fortunately for him there was so much to begin with that no one has really cared, until now. Daddy has finally noticed. He is going to disinherit him. This is rumoured but not confirmed. He is married to the glamourous Dolores.

Dolores
Dolores is a really talented actress. She really resents that no one takes her seriously anymore because of her association with JJP 111 and the stories about JJP Senior buying her the role that made her famous. Now "Serious" Directors won't touch her.

Julia
Wants to be the next democratic candidate for President of the USA. She is feisty and well informed and a warrior for climate change. No one knows why she has accepted the invitation to JJP's Mansion (arranged by Rafe, apparently), except that her family are old money, and all the old money families hang out...Turns out...She really is a climate change warrior. JJP's factories world-wide have been pouring out carbon and he refuses to change. She has come along with Rafe.

Please make sure that you know who is who, or it's going to get a bit complicated.

At Card 3 you will be handed a card in an envelope and be invited to open it. It will tell you if you are the killer or not. Whatever it says is private to you. If you are the killer, you can be as deceptive as you wish. Essentially everyone has alibis, and they all have holes in. JJP11 was murdered at his desk. Poisoned and then bashed on the head. This happened at some point in the afternoon when you were all enjoying his hospitality (Irena, of course, lives at West Egg anyway).

I hope this all works out! But if it does get a bit complicated, we have good food, wine and company anyway!

Quick Original Cast List

John J Pilaster 111	Dabs
Dolores Everhartt	Giselle
Tony Biblioni	Gareth
Carlotta Borlotti	Fi
Rafe Hardy	Paul
Julia Detvarmeg	Bev
Hamish McHammer	Dids
Irena Alexandrovna Yaetosdelal	Jo

When everyone digs into their oysters, the "host" is apparently sleeping at his desk ... Nobody has the nerve to wake him...

A little more guidance before the day.

Preparation.

You must prepare yourself by being familiar with your character's back story. Ideally you should try and dress the part. The action is set in 1926 in the Gatsby Mansion at West Egg on Long Island, New York.

You should not discuss your story with your partner. They

must not know of your particular secret re the Pilaster Family. They will only know that you have met them before, socially, through business or because of some dispute.

On arrival. All characters.

Over aperitifs

Make sure that you chat to the people that you don't know. Everyone must tell the truth about their basic background, except Tony Biblioni who is a "businessman" operating out of the West Side.

You should all be asking how the others know JJ Pilaster 11, putting a positive light on your relationship.

You only need to be in character when Tony Biblioni is wearing his glasses. Otherwise, just chat and enjoy.

Individual questions to ask and hints at responses will be in your laminated question bundles in order (included). Keep these to yourselves. You can also improvise and try and catch people out. In each round you will either be required to ask a question or to respond. You can ask questions of your own to probe alibis or, at the end, to accuse people.

Please don't feel any stress. We are here to have fun and if you stumble over a question or a response, it doesn't matter at all.

The Big Reveal

When Tony Biblioni asks the group who the murderer is, stand dramatically {or at least sit up straight} and say what it says on you card...

I've written 8 different solutions and I won't know which one is in play until the final envelope is opened...

As host you could also try:
Give everyone a killer card, so they all did it ... or
Get a friend in costume to hide in the house (somewhere nice with a drink and some food) so that they can appear at the right moment as JJP11, who has survived all the attempts to kill him and isn't aware that they have tried!

Invitations are on the next page, laid out for copying

Dear Guest,

As you may have heard, Jay Gatsby has "departed".

I have bought his lavish mansion at West Egg on Long Island, complete with the view, where you will be having dinner on the evening of August 28th[th], 1926.

My slightly lesser Industrial Giant than me, son, John J Pilaster 111, a Pillar of Long Island Society, and his glamorous second wife, the film star, Dolores Everhartt, will be looking after you before dinner.

Please arrive by mid-day, change in your rooms and enjoy yourselves; swimming, playing tennis, boating on the lake, walking in the woods etc.

I will be upstairs in my suite should you wish to put your head around the door, but I will be busy making many more millions. I do occasionally powernap, so don't be surprised if I am sleeping at my desk.

Please gather in the secret garden for Champagne, Brandy Old Fashion's and hors d'oeuvres, in appropriate evening wear, at 6pm.

Yours in anticipation,

John J Pilaster 11,
(Industrial Giant and Pillar of Society)

Hamish McHammer
You are invited to a
Grand Dinner
Please gather at 4pm for Canapes
and
Suitable Drinks
Smart Fashionable Attire
August 28th, 1926

John J Pilaster 11

John J Pilaster 111

Your playing age is the age you are, conveniently.

You are the son and heir of the Multi-Billionaire John J Pilaster 11.

You went to an expensive private school in Scotland {Gordonstoun} so you could hang out with the Royals.

This also meant that he could check out his Golf courses there {or get you to, if he couldn't make it over}. All of which are very exclusive and losing money. He had lots of Scots evicted to create these!

Daddy bought you a place at Harvard where you sort of completed a degree in Business.

It didn't do you any good and ever since you took over the family business you have been losing money steadily. To begin with, fortunately for you, there was so much to begin with that no-one noticed, but now Daddy has, and he is threatening to cut you off!

So, you are here with Dolores Everhartt, your wife.

Dolores Everhartt

Your playing age is whichever age you are, give or take, which is convenient.

You are one of the Great Romantic Film Stars of the Age. When you were 18 you were suddenly promoted from the chorus after a party at West Egg, where you had accompanied Rafe Hardy.

Now film roles fell into your lap and you found yourself making Light Romance after Light Romance, but never anything that would give you a chance to show how talented you are!

Eventually, you became the girlfriend of and then married John J Pilaster 111 and Semi-Retired into a life of Luxury. Now you have discovered that your "break" was financed by JJ Senior, that everyone knew it but you and that THAT was why you lost out on the Leading Roles to Clara Bow every time!

You are not very HAPPY about that, but have concealed your annoyance, until now....

So, you are here with JJP 111

John J Pilaster 111 and Dolores Everhartt

Anthony Biblioni

Your playing age is whatever age you are, which is convenient.

You are an aspiring New York Gangster, known as "Tony the Book".

This is because you launder the mob's money through bookshops and on-line sales. Selling very cheap books at very high prices so you get the excessive "agents" share of the massive royalties in clean money.

This has made you very rich and powerful.

You are very protective of your beautiful girlfriend "Carlotta Borlotti", and you know that John J Pilaster 11 blocked her career in favour of Dolores Everhartt.

Honour is honour and an insult to your girlfriend is an insult to you.

The question is, how far would you go to take your revenge?

So, you are here with Carlotta Borlotti.

Carlotta Borlotti

Your playing age is whichever age you are, give or take, which is convenient.

You are deeply resentful of the influence JJP 11 brought to bear to get Dolores the part that made her famous, a part that you think you should have got. Sometimes you can't help but mention this.

As it was, after that failed audition, you fell into ever more "characterful" roles, mostly as Gangsters molls.

It was in such a role that you met Tony, who had been cast by Martin Scorsese' and Coppola' Grandads in yet another re-working of "Gangsters of New York", in return for "permission" to make the film at all.

He "persuaded" you to retire from the movies and now you mostly live in a world of shopping and cocktail parties.

So, you are here with Tony Biblioni.

Tony Biblioni and Julia Detvarmeg

Rafe Hardy

Your playing age is whichever age you are, give or take, which is convenient.

Public school educated from a wealthy background, you worked briefly in the city then launched into a "career" as a writer and an actor.

Your mother, an American heiress, was a relation of JJP 11 and it was his publishing and film companies that guaranteed your successes.

You think that this is fine and nothing more than your due. You were slightly annoyed when Dolores, who met JJP 111 through you, went on to marry him.

Tony Biblioni is trying to buy the rights to all of your books, and you don't know why.

You are sure though that he isn't quite the ticket...

You are here with Julia Detvarmeg, who asked you to arrange her invitation as a favour... You smell a story.

Julia Detvarmeg

You are playing age is whichever age you are, give or take, which is convenient.

You are a Democratic Senator for the state of Vermont.
You have been invited because JJP 111 needs democratic support for a new factory and he been funding your campaigns.

What he hasn't realised, until your last speech, is that you have been converted to the cause of stopping climate change and have had a huge telegram row with JJP 11 about his factories and mines pouring out CO_2 and destroying rainforests. JJP 11 has cut off your funding!

You have come to the conclusion that he will never listen to you and that he will always put profit first.

Your name, in Norwegian, means "it was me", which is a secret, or is it... You are here with Rafe Hardy. You asked him to arrange it as a "favour".

Hamish McHammer and Irena Yaetosdelal

Hamish McHammer

You became famous when you won the largest ever Lottery win and not spending it because you have everything that you need. You are invited everywhere to see if you can be tempted.

HOWEVER, you are in disguise.

You are the ex-butler of JJP 11, the victim. He found you working, as a butler, in a luxury Golf Course Hotel in Scotland and made you an offer you couldn't refuse. You mysteriously disappeared several years later when you had the win.

What he didn't know was that your family croft was bulldozed after being compulsory purchased for a pittance (which was never paid anyway) to build that very golf course and you have been seething ever since.

You are very familiar with the layout of the house, something which you must conceal…

You are here with Irena. She invited you out of the blue and you "don't know" the others.

Irena Alexandrova Yaetosdelal

Your playing age is whichever age you are, give or take, which is convenient.

You are the mistress of the deceased, put aside when he realised that your collection of Faberge Eggs, which he wanted for his West Egg Mansion, had been lost on the Titanic! You became the "Queen" of West Egg, but otherwise you have largely been largely ignored for a long time. Greta Garbo will base her screen persona on you. You often want to be alone.

This evening you have invited Hamish McHammer to dinner because your ex-lover, JJP 11, often ignores you. You think Hamish is familiar, but you can't place him. Is it just because he was on the cover of "Time" when he had his massive lottery win? Or is there something else?

Rafe Hardy and Carlotta Borlotti

This next section contains the questions that each character should ask and the answers they can give, when prompted by the host, who should be Tony Biblioni.

Remember, only the murderer is allowed to lie, but anyone can ask additional questions or give extra information.

The pages are laid out to making printing and cutting easy. In the original version the character initials were written on the back of each card, and each page was laminated before it was cut.

John J Pilaster 111

Ask Hamish if he plays golf when he's in Scotland. 1	Respond to the discovery of the body with "horror". Agree with Tony when he says that no-one wants the Police involved. Say, "I don't want anyone suggesting I did the old man in! It certainly wasn't me! 2
Open your envelope. Be "poker faced" about the content. If you are the Killer, you can lie. If you are not you can make up answers but not to deliberately incriminate yourself. 3	When asked by Tony for an alibi, say: "Dolores was all taken up with Rafe so I took the boat out into the bay, ended up dropping in to see Daisy over in East Egg. Turns out they had already left for the coast, but anybody could have seen me in my boat". 4
The next 4 rounds are about asking probing questions to try and discover the truth (or hide it if you are the killer!). You can use the questions and responses on the cards or make up your own. REMEMBER, if you are the killer you should be trying to misdirect people! 5	Ask Irene if she and "Daddy" are getting on any better after the last argument. 6

When asked by Tony if it's OK to disrespect a woman say: "No, No way. I man like that doesn't deserve to live". 7	When Hamish comments on how much your manservant looks like you, say: "Oh. Do you really think so? No-one has ever mentioned that before. He's welsh you know". 8
When asked by Carlotta how the Alaskan Pipeline Project and about money, say: "It's not so bad. I'm told Trump wants to buy in. Anyway, Daddy was cool about it!" 9	This is when you can make accusations. You don't need to do this in character. Have you noticed any inconsistencies or picked up on a motive? Can you back up what you say? if not, just pick on someone! 10
If you are not the Killer: When the killer reveals themselves react with mock horror for a moment then say: "Yeah, he did." After, "Blame". 11	When prompted by Tony say: "He had it coming He had it coming He only had himself to blame. Yes! I am the Killer! I paid a guy to drive the boat around wearing my hat, so I had plenty of time to slip him some poison AND to bash him on the back of the head! He was gonna cut me off and no self-respecting rich guy could put up with that! Now, who wants a drink! 12

Dolores Everhartt

When asked if you expect the role of Camille, answer that that B***H Crawford will get it. No one takes me seriously as an actress. And why should they after what HE did! (If pushed reveal that JJP11 bought you your first starring role as a gift for his son). 1	Respond to the discovery of the body with "horror". Agree with Tony when he says that no-one wants the Police involved. 2
Open your envelope. Be "poker faced" about the content. If you are the Killer, you can lie. If you are not you can make up answers but not to deliberately incriminate yourself. 3	When Tony asks you for an alibi, say: "I was with Rafe in the Summerhouse, we talked about a book about a Great Actress who was never really appreciated as a talent because of her beauty and the wealth of her family, who SOME people believe is why she gets the parts." (glare at Carlotta). 4
The next 4 rounds are about asking probing questions to try and discover the truth (or hide it if you are the killer!). You can use the questions and responses on the cards or make up your own. REMEMBER, if you are the killer you should be trying to misdirect people! 5	Ask Carlotta if she thinks the role of a Gangsters Moll is right for an actress of "her calibre". 6

When Irena asks you why you came the wrong way to her bedroom say: "Ah, yes, I used the other stairs so that I could check on the caterers, that's all…". 7	Say to Tony: "Mr Biblioni, I happened to be in one of your "bookshops" the other day. I noticed that there was a very big section of Detective novels". 8
Say to Hamish: "You was talking of likenesses Mr McHammer. I just can't shake the feeling that I've seen you somewhere before. You just look so familiar!" 9	This is when you can make accusations. You don't need to do this in character. Have you noticed any inconsistencies or picked up on a motive? Can you back up what you say? if not, just pick on someone! 10
If you are not the Killer: When the killer reveals themselves react with mock horror for a moment then say: "Yeah, he did." After, "Blame". 11	When prompted by Tony say: "He had it coming He had it coming He only had himself to blame. So! It was me! And who can blame me! He ruined my career when he treated me like a handbag for his "boy". When Rafe fell asleep, it was easy to slip away and slip poison to the old coot! Now who wants a drink! 12

30

Antony {Tony} Biblioni

When asked by Rafe how busines is going, tell him "very well, particularly on The West Side, but it's a long story. 1	Go to see what's keeping JJP11. Come back shocked because you have found him slumped over his desk with an empty glass in his hand and a lump on his head. Say "I think the old man is dead. I can't detect any breathing. This is bad. I can't be having any Police here. What do you'se guys think? OK, I'm gonna lead the investigation. Anybody got a problem with that? But first, let's eat" 2
Open your envelope. Be "poker faced" about the content. If you are the Killer, you can lie. If you are not you can make up answers but not to deliberately incriminate yourself. 3	Say: "We needs to eliminate everyone that has a cast iron cover story, I mean alibi. I'm gonna asks you where's you've been all afternoon, and you'se is gonna tell me straight. Got it? Good" Now ask each character for their alibi. Challenge Hamish that he has no alibi 4
The next 4 rounds are about asking probing questions to try and discover the truth (or hide it if you are the killer!). You can use the questions and responses on the cards or make up your own. REMEMBER, if you are the killer you should be trying to misdirect people! 5	Say: "Hey Hamish ... Earlier when you offered to refresh my Scotch, you seemed to know exactly where to go? Why is that?" When Julia says that violence is never the answer, say: "You can say that, but it can depend on the question". 6

Ask JJP111 if he thinks it's OK in this day and age for a man to treat a woman without respect. 7	When Dolores comments on the large Detective section in your bookshop say: "That's true Lady. It is a genre that we specialises in. Keeps us one step ahead, so to speak. Easy on the wine please". 8
Say to Rafe: Hey, Rafe, have you thought about my "offer" to buy the rights to all of yuose books? 9	This is when you can make accusations. You don't need to do this in character. Have you noticed any inconsistencies or picked up on a motive? Can you back up what you say? if not, just pick on someone! 10
If you are not the Killer: When the killer reveals themselves react with mock horror for a moment then say: "Yeah, he did." After, "Blame". 11	At the right moment say: He had it coming He had it coming He only had himself to blame. Yes, it was me! Tony Biblioni, Book Loving Mafiosi! And who could blame me! You? You? I thought not. He done my girl a great disservice, and in my world, that ain't gonna happen twice. Carlotta spends so much time on her preparations for dinner that it was easy to slip away and do the deed! Now, who wants a drink! 12

Carlotta Borlotti

Ask Dolores whether she expects to get the role of "Camille" in this year's big movie 1	Respond to the discovery of the body with "horror". Agree with Tony when he says that no-one wants the Police involved. It would ruin your career. 2
Open your envelope. Be "poker faced" about the content. If you are the Killer, you can lie. If you are not you can make up answers but not to deliberately incriminate yourself. 3	When I asked by Tony to provide an alibi, say, "But Tony, you of all people should know where I was. WE was on the lake in a canoe, canoodling...all of the afternoon. 4
The next 4 rounds are about asking probing questions to try and discover the truth (or hide it if you are the killer!). You can use the questions and responses on the cards or make up your own. REMEMBER, if you are the killer you should be trying to misdirect people! 5	When asked a question by Dolores, respond. "Well, it can be useful, in matters of honour...Oh, you mean in the movies... 6

Say to Julia: "I do so admire a woman who is prepared to take on the most powerful men in the world for a cause she believes in". 7	To Irena, say: "Remind us, Irena, how you came to be the Queen of West Egg. It's such a romantic story!" 8
Say to JJP 111: "Say, JJ, how are things going with the Alaskan Pipeline Project, only I heard that the plans had all been put on hold and you were losing a great deal of money with every passing day? How did Daddy feel about that?" When he replies say: "He certainly is now, and cooler by the minute". 9	This is when you can make accusations. You don't need to do this in character. Have you noticed any inconsistencies or picked up on a motive? Can you back up what you say? if not, just pick on someone! 10
If you are not the Killer: When the killer reveals themselves react with mock horror for a moment then say: "Yeah, he did." After, "Blame". 11	When prompted by Tony say: "He had it coming He had it coming He only had himself to blame". So, I am the killer! But he sure had it coming! If he hadn't bought Dolores those early leads, I could have been a Great Star, and not have ended up playing a gangster's moll! (No offence Tony). We did go canoodling for a while, but there was plenty of time whilst everyone was changing for dinner to do the deed. Now, who wants a drink? 12

Rafe Hardy

Ask Tony how things are going in the bookselling business. 1	Respond to the discovery of the body with "horror". Agree with Tony when he says that no-one wants the Police involved. 2
Open your envelope. Be "poker faced" about the content. If you are the Killer, you can lie. If you are not you can make up answers but not to deliberately incriminate yourself. 3	When Tony asks you for an alibi and Dolores has told her story, say: "It's true, at least it's mostly true, we were discussing such a book, but we came to no decision ... then. But I have though, now, and the answer is... frankly my dear ... No. AND, I did drift off after the second rerun of your life story, so you could have been gone a while". 4
The next 4 rounds are about asking probing questions to try and discover the truth (or hide it if you are the killer!). You can use the questions and responses on the cards or make up your own. REMEMBER, if you are the killer you should be trying to misdirect people! 5	Ask Julia if you can shadow her to research your new book about an environmental campaigner who turns to violence. 6

When asked a question by Hamish, reply. "Sales are Just fine, thank you Mr McHammer. Couldn't be better". Make sure you sound bitter. 7	To Julia, say: "You know, Ms Detvarmeg, I learned Norwegian once for a film role. I suppose you must know that Det var Meg in that language means ... "It was me!" 8
When Tony asks you if he can buy the rights to all of your books say: "I was expecting that. Since JJ's better offer is now "off the table". You're not someone that someone says no to Tony, so it's a yes from me. 9	This is when you can make accusations. You don't need to do this in character. Have you noticed any inconsistencies or picked up on a motive? Can you back up what you say? if not, just pick on someone! 10
If you are not the Killer: When the killer reveals themselves react with mock horror for a moment then say: "Yeah, he did." After "Blame". 11	When prompted by Tony say: "He had it coming He had it coming He only had himself to blame. So, I am the killer! It was easy to pretend to snooze so that Dolores would wander off. And then I bashed him with his own bible! I could have been a real writer if I wasn't born into money and privilege! But now I'll never know. Who wants a drink? 12

Julia Detvarmeg

Ask Irena if she is comfortable in such a large house, bought with oil money. 1	Respond to the discovery of the body with "horror". Agree with Tony when he says that no-one wants the Police involved. 2
Open your envelope. Be "poker faced" about the content. If you are the Killer, you can lie. If you are not you can make up answers but not to deliberately incriminate yourself. 3	When asked for an alibi by Tony, say, "I was taking calls from Washington all afternoon about important world stuff. It should be easy to check, we all know that all our calls recorded by the FBI, and if that fails, try the Russians." 4
The next 4 rounds are about asking probing questions to try and discover the truth (or hide it if you are the killer!). You can use the questions and responses on the cards or make up your own. REMEMBER, if you are the killer you should be trying to misdirect people! 5	When asked by Rafe if he can shadow you to research his new book about an environmental campaigner who turns to violence. Say pointedly that VIOLENCE IS NEVER THE ANSWER. 6

When Carlotta talks about admiring you say: "Being a woman doesn't come into it. When it comes to saving the planet from these people, there isn't much that I wouldn't do". 7	When Rafe reveals the meaning of your name say: "But Mr Hardy, you can't hold that against me! If you knew better than film Norwegian, you would know that "Det Var" is "The Spring" and "Meg" simply me. A testament to my green credentials! 8
When Irena asks you about your campaign funds say, icily: "They're just fine thank you. The Kennedy's have stepped up. They can see the future is blowin in the wind. 9	This is when you can make accusations. You don't need to do this in character. Have you noticed any inconsistencies or picked up on a motive? Can you back up what you say? if not, just pick on someone! 10
If you are not the Killer: When the killer reveals themselves react with mock horror for a moment then say: "Yeah, he did." After "Blame". 11	When prompted by Tony say: "He had it coming He had it coming He only had himself to blame". So, I am the Killer! Even though I am a Representative of the People of this Great Nation! He just would not listen to reason and the World just had to be saved from his Disastrous Industrial Developments. I mean, what's wrong with these people? Oh, the phone calls? Pre-recorded, of course. Now, who wants a drink! 12

Hamish McHammer

When asked if you play golf, answer along the lines of, "I'm a hammer man me-self, as my name implies. Golf's a wee game for rich people. 1	Respond to the discovery of the body with "horror". Agree with Tony when he says that no-one wants the Police involved. 2
Open your envelope. Be "poker faced" about the content. If you are the Killer, you can lie. If you are not you can make up answers but not to deliberately incriminate yourself. 3	When asked by Tony for an alibi, say: "I was walking in the woods looking for any potential cabers. There's not much left in Scotland now, what with all the golf courses being built!" When Tony challenges you with having no alibi, say: "Och, I wouldna know when end of a blunt instrument from the other. You've no need to be looking at little old me!" 4
The next 4 rounds are about asking probing questions to try and discover the truth (or hide it if you are the killer!). You can use the questions and responses on the cards or make up your own. REMEMBER, if you are the killer you should be trying to misdirect people! 5	When asked a question by Tony, explain that you were interested in buying the house, so you looked at the plans on Zoopla. 6

Ask Rafe "How have your book sales been doing ... since Maamy died." I suppose JJ has been looking after you!" 7	To JJP 111: "I saw your manservant down by the jetty earlier this afternoon. It's amazing how much he looks like you, from a distance, of course?" 8
When Dolores talks about you looking familiar say: "Have you ever been to your Boyfriends Golf Course at Turnberry? I have a lot of family in that area and all of us are very close with strong family ties!" 9	This is when you can make accusations. You don't need to do this in character. Have you noticed any inconsistencies or picked up on a motive? Can you back up what you say? if not, just pick on someone! 10
If you are not the Killer: When the killer reveals themselves react with mock horror for a moment then say: "Yeah, he did." After, "Blame". 11	When prompted by Tony say: "He had it coming He had it coming He only had himself to blame. Aye, "I am the killer! And he had it coming!" He stole my wee Daddies croft to use as the 18th hole on his swanky golf course and paid him ner a penny! Och, and I was his Butler here for years and none of you recognised me! 12

Irena Yaetosdelal

When asked, answer that you are as comfortable as can be expected in such a tiny place where there are so few servants, and your lover is so rarely to be seen. 1	Respond to the discovery of the body with "horror". Agree with Tony when he says that no-one wants the Police involved. 2
Open your envelope. Be "poker faced" about the content. If you are the Killer, you can lie. If you are not you can make up answers but not to deliber6ately incriminate yourself. 3	When asked for your story by Tony, say: "I drifted around the grounds for a while, then took to my chaise-longue. I vanted to be alone, you see." Tony will say then that you have no Alibi. Reply: "Ah, but my chaise-longue is in the bay window, visible to all who care to look up!" 4
The next 4 rounds are about asking probing questions to try and discover the truth (or hide it if you are the killer!). You can use the questions and responses on the cards or make up your own. REMEMBER, if you are the killer you should be trying to misdirect people! 5	When asked by JJP111 if you are getting on any better after your last argument with JJP11, reply, "It's difficult to tell. I see very little of him and when I do see him, he is usually drunk. 6

Ask Dolores: "Darling, this afternoon I asked you to bring my book to my room. You did, but your footsteps came from the wrong way? From the direction of JJ's study? Why was that? 7	When Carlotta asks you how you came to be the "Queen of West Egg", say: Ah, my dear, JJ, no longer with us, was at a dinner party where I was also a guest. He wooed me and I moved in here. Turns out he had heard of my fabulous collection of Faberge Eggs and he asked me to bring them to New York. He paid for their passage, but it was on the Titanic! When the Eggs went down, so did his ardour ... but I stayed on ever hopeful ... 8
Say to Julia: "Julia, how are your campaign funds looking, after the last email from JJP11. Looks like he'd decided to pull out of windfarms AND that the Republicans were a better bet after that carbon neutral speech of yours and wanted his money back". 9	This is when you can make accusations. You don't need to do this in character. Have you noticed any inconsistencies or picked up on a motive? Can you back up what you say? if not, just pick on someone! 10
If you are not the Killer: When the killer reveals themselves react with mock horror for a moment then say: "Yeah, he did." After, "Blame". 11	When prompted by Tony say: "He had it coming He had it coming He only had himself to blame. So, it was me! And who can blame me! Locked away in his dusty mansions for years. Just another part of his collection! A mannikin dressed as me on the chaise-longue was all it took! And a good dose of poison! Now, who wants a drink? 12

Sample Menu (as served at the original dinner)

A fine dinner at West Egg
October 9th, 1926
Menu
Gin and Tonic on arrival
§
Oysters Rockefeller or Fig and Sultana Toasts Rockefeller
Champagne cocktail
§
Devilled Eggs
Brandy Old Fashioned sweet cocktail
§
Garden-fresh cocktail with Seafood or Feta
Two Bottles of 19 Crimes Chardonnay 2020
§
Rose wine sorbet
§
Beef or Vegetarian Wellington
Dauphinoise potatoes
A medley of vegetables
Two Bottles of Saint-Émilion Grand Cru,
Château Abelyce 2016
§
Lemon posset
De Bortoli Dessert Semillon 2017
§
Cheese and Biscuits
Symington Family Estate Late Bottled Port, 2015
§
Coffee and Chocolates with a good selection of Spirits
Some of them fine...

You are the Killer! Good Luck!	You are not the killer but keep this to yourself!
You are not the killer but keep this to yourself!	You are not the killer but keep this to yourself!
You are not the killer but keep this to yourself!	You are not the killer but keep this to yourself!
You are not the killer but keep this to yourself!	You are not the killer but keep this to yourself!

Also by Gareth Jones

Non-Fiction

On This Day for Teachers

Saving the Planet, one step at a time {as "Plays in the Rain"}

Dealer's Choice, The Home Poker Game Handbook

Mametz Wood, Three Stories of Wales {First published by Bretwalda}

Outstanding School Trip Leadership

Top Teacher Tips for Outstanding Behaviour for Learning {as Gethin James}

Cheeky Elf Solutions for Busy Parents

A Short Report on the Planet known locally as Earth {as Abel Star}

Make Your Own Teepee

Travelling with Children {First published by Bretwalda. Now in its second edition and fully illustrated}

Identifying Gifted and Talented Children, and what to do next

Outstanding Transition, A Teacher's Guide

An Unofficial set of revision notes for the Edexcel GCSE, History B, American West

An Unofficial set of revision notes for the Edexcel GCSE, History B, Medicine Unit

The Big Activity Book for KS3 Drama {published by ZigZag}

The Drama Handbook KS2 {this is an age adapted version of the above. They should not be bought together}

Personal Learning Project Guide {March 2020}

The Tower of Hanoi {The 127 Solution}

Short Stories

The Christmas Owls {Based on an idea by Millie C}

The Pheasant that Refused to Fly {includes "The Cave." Winner of the 2018 Hailsham Arts Festival Short Story Competition}

The Unicorns of Moons Hill and the Broken Heart {Based on an idea by Millie C}

An Owl called Moonlight and The Midnight Tree {Based on an idea by Millie C}

The Amazing Adventures of Edwina Elf {Based on an idea by Millie C}
A Mermacorn Christmas Adventure {Based on an idea by Millie C}
"A Shirt for Mr De Niro" and other Stories
Hailsham Festival Anthology 2019 {Edited by}
Hailsham Festival Anthology 2020 {Edited by}
Hailsham Festival Anthology 2021 {Edited by}
Mollie's Midnight Adventure with the Magical Moon Magician
The Valley of the Rainbows

Plays

Georgina and the Dragon {First published by Schoolplay}
Jason and the Astronauts {Also first published by Schoolplay}
Pelias Strikes Back! {The sequel to Jason}
William Shakespeare's Romeo and Juliet, A new adaption for KS2 and KS3
Dr Milo's Experiment
GET SANTA! From the original East Sussex film project
The Space Pirate Panto
Cinderella and the Raiders of the Lost Slipper {includes "Goldilocks", the full story}
William Tell, The Panto

Novels

Heartsong
Get Santa: The Novel
When the Romans Came

Undefinable

Short Stories and Plot Outlines that would make GREAT FILMS, Mr Steven Spielberg, Sir
Quick Comedy Sketches for Young Comedians {as performed at "The Paragon Spectacular, White Rock Theatre, Hastings}
The Quiz That Keeps on Giving. A Charity Fund Raiser
JPR Williams X-Rayed my Head